The Magic Box

By Stephen L. Conroy

Illustrated by Jason Pope

Elfin Cove Press
1481 130th Avenue NE
Bellevue, WA 98005
www.elfincovepress.com

The Magic Box

Project manager: Bernie Ornelas
Cover Design & Illustrations: Jason Pope
Text Design: Amy Peloff
Editors: Diane Hendrix, Bernie Ornelas, and Stephen L. Conroy

ISBN 0944958-25-7
Library of Congress 2002114629
Printed in Korea
1 3 5 7 9 10 8 6 4 2

To my family:

Rosemary, Meghan, Jake, and Casey Clare

"Imagination is more important than knowledge"

– Albert Einstein, age 75

"Oh Daddy, what imaginations you have!"

– Meghan O'Shaughnessey Conroy, age 5

More adventures of

Paddy Cornelius O'Shaughnessey

can be found in

There Must Be Magic in This House

ISBN 0944958-30-3

More titles will follow!

The Magic Box

By Stephen L. Conroy

Illustrated by Jason Pope

Chapter One

Once There Was Once Upon a Time
a Great Battle and a Magic Box

Once upon a time long, long ago, in a faraway land, there was a Magic Box. It was quite an ordinary looking box, none too particular, none too pretty, but it contained fantastic magical powers for whoever possessed it. For the one who owned that box could use its power to influence the sun, the moon and the stars; to direct the rain and the wind; and to control the sea, the rivers and the mountains. The owner of the box had control over all the land.

When used properly and wisely, the magic in this magic box could make the land bountiful and its entire people happy and prosperous. Fortunately for those who lived in this faraway land of long ago, a gnome king beloved by all of his subjects, aptly named Good King Brendon, owned the Magic Box. When he used the powers of the Magic Box (which was rarely), he used them wisely. This was not just a land of gnomes, unicorns, wizards, fairies and all beings good and wonderful, however…this land also harbored an evil presence.

Bordering Good King Brendon's kingdom was the Raging River. This river was wild and treacherous, too dangerous to cross, even with the most sturdy and dependable

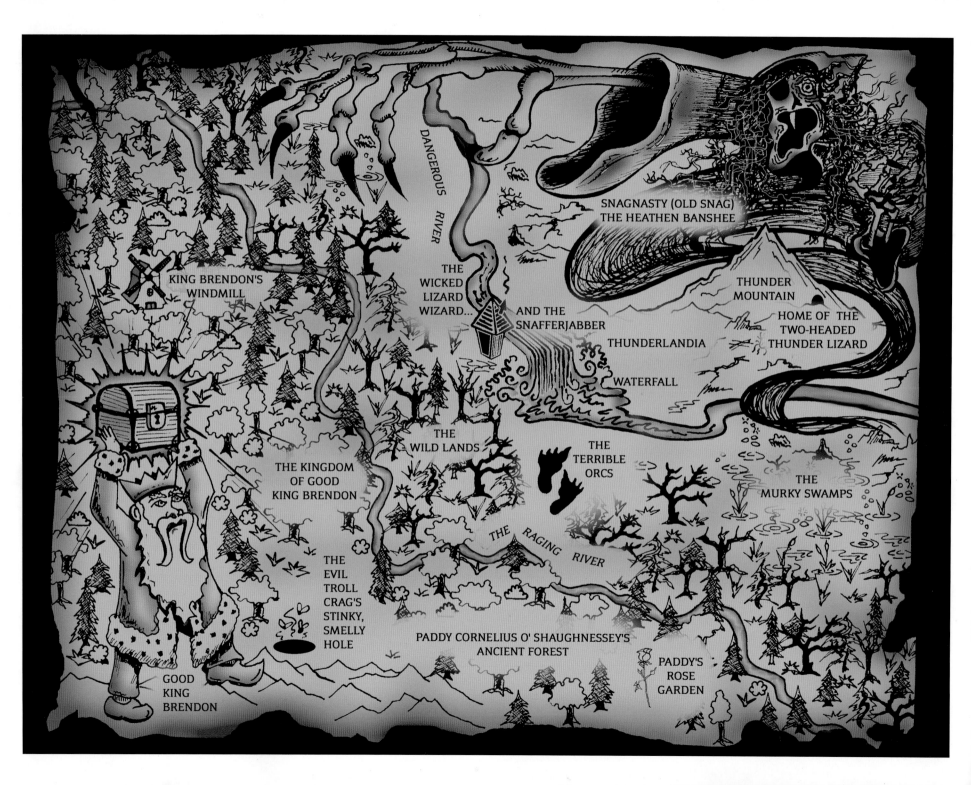

of boats. As luck would have it, the Raging River divided the land, separating good from evil. At times, Good King Brendon used all of his efforts and energies, along with the magic contained in the Magic Box, to keep the evil at bay, and on the other side of this Raging River.

Across the Raging River were the Wild Lands. Those lands were a terrible place indeed, and dangerous for even a gnome—even Good King Brendon. Trolls, orcs and other nasty and despicable creatures inhabited the Wild Lands, but that was not the half of it. Beyond the Wild Lands were the murky swamps—home to poisonous snakes, warty toads, sewer rats, mangy polecats and other unspeakable vermin that slimed and slithered. This was a most dangerous place for a good soul to wander (especially a gnome), because the mongrel beasts that called this place home were sworn enemies of gnomes and all they stood for.

Finally, and worst of all, beyond the murky swamps was a cold and dark patch of the world known as Thunderlandia. This was the pit of the earth. The mountains there were ragged spikes, which twisted angrily into a black sky. The land itself was barren and desolate—dead really—and one Wicked Lizard Wizard roamed its borders. This was a place no gnome or sensible person dared go. Thunderlandia was a truly evil and inhospitable place.

At the far, bitter end of Thunderlandia stood Thunder Mountain. This was a rugged, ugly piece of rock, the lair of the two-headed monster called the Thunder Lizard. The Thunder Lizard guarded the gold and riches of the most malevolent being

in this entire faraway land of long ago. That wicked, awful creature was the Heathen Banshee, an old hag named Snagnasty (whose name was spoken softly, if at all), who was called at times, simply, Old Snag.

The Heathen Banshee was vile and mean spirited, full of hatred and spite. She was nasty to the very core, and in fact she had only one tooth in her miserable head. That was even said to be rotten, as rotten as she was. The Heathen Banshee was always up to no good, scheming evil deeds. Of course, she coveted the Magic Box and the powers it contained.

The Heathen Banshee was vile and mean spirited, full of hatred and spite...

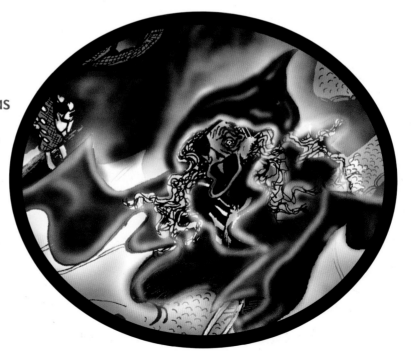

At one time the Heathen Banshee did possess the Magic Box. Then she was a powerful queen who viciously ruled this faraway land and held the ancestors of the Good King Brendon captive as lowly serfs and slaves. Snagnasty had a fearless army of brutal warriors who ruthlessly defended her territory. Old Snag regularly declared war and sent her minions into battle, constantly overthrowing the forces of good. So malicious was her hard heart, and so persistent her desire to conquer good, that the ancient gnome king was eventually forced to confront her force with rebellion.

A ragged band of brave gnome warriors attacked Old Snag's castle in a valiant and surprising uprising, plundering her castle and seizing the Magic Box. Seizing the box reversed the battle, for without the Magic Box, Snagnasty had no power. She and her army of bullies turned tail and ran. Without the secrets of the box, they were seen for what they were: cowards.

The Good King Brendon, who at the time was a foot soldier in the ancient gnome king's ragtag army, fought the Heathen Banshee face to face on the battlements of her castle with sword and dagger, in full view of her archers and lancers. Eventually gaining the advantage, Brendon poked out one of the Heathen Banshee's evil eyes with his dagger, leaving a bloody hole. Even today the old crone wears a patch to hide the blind eye, its dead socket glazed over with a nasty gray film, perpetually oozing pus.

When wounded, the Old Snag shrieked in pain; and her cowardly soldiers, upon seeing their cruel leader injured, grew disoriented and fled. The gnomes then forced what was left of the Heathen Banshee's minions to retreat across the Raging River, where

many were lost to the treacherous current. Eventually, the hag took refuge with what was left of her bedraggled army in the bleak caverns and dark places beneath Thunder Mountain, bringing with her a hoard of gold, diamonds, rubies and other precious jewels.

To this very day in this faraway land, the Heathen Banshee—comforted only by her riches—remains in the bowels of Thunder Mountain, where the Two-Headed Thunder Lizard protects her. Her pets, the Fearless Vampire Bats (the most evil creatures to take wing in this faraway land), hang at all entries, posted as guards to the interior of the mountain. Old Snag whiles away her days wandering the depths of Thunder Mountain in desolation and despair. A miserable and wretched creature whose only goal was to wreak havoc and destruction everywhere, she treated every living thing with cruelty. Bored, she began to plot the theft of the Magic Box from the Good King Brendon in order to use its secrets for her black magic.

No gnome had ever been to Thunder Mountain, besides those warriors who drove the Heathen Banshee into its caverns so many years ago. It was unthinkable to consider going there, when the other half of this faraway land, ruled by the Good King Brendon, was so beautiful and prosperous.

Good King Brendon's domain was a land of ancient forests, giant trees, flower laden meadows, clear blue lakes and babbling brooks, where the woods were full of chatter and all creatures lived in harmony. And so it was that most, if not all, of those who inhabited the kingdom of the Good King Brendon never gave Thunderlandia or the Heathen Banshee a second thought.

The kingdom enjoyed such peace and prosperity that it was difficult to imagine that such evil lay just across a river. And because the Good King Brendon used the Magic Box wisely, there was never a cause for his subjects, particularly his faithful gnomes, to venture across the Raging River to the dark land beyond.

Still, the Heathen Banshee continued to lust after the Magic Box. Over the years her greed became more and more intense. She was consumed daily by just one thought: how to recapture the box and use its powers for her own ends. So determined was this miserable hag, that every night she flipped up the patch on her evil eye and stared into her cracked mirror. She used the hypnotic power of her dead eye to convince herself that she was invincible. Often she actually saw herself holding the box in her gnarled, warty hands. But all too often, her wizardry backfired, and Old Snag only put herself into a trance, which leaked terror into her wicked heart. Each time this happened, after snapping out of her trance, she'd find herself in a foul mood, curse her fate and promise revenge against the Good King Brendon.

Day after day, the greedy and mean-spirited Heathen Banshee paced the caves and dead spots under Thunder Mountain, seething with wickedness and frustration. She played again and again in her mind's eye the grand battle when her demon warriors were subdued and her castle destroyed, transformed into rubble. Her worst nightmare came when she had to flee with her gold, like a coward, to the most wretched place on earth, Thunder Mountain. This desolate spot was a far cry from her grand castle and palace. Inevitably she would recall her fateful encounter with the warrior gnome, remembering how he poked out her eye, leaving an ugly oozing sore, a gaping sightless ball of pus in its socket. At these times, Snagnasty plotted using her evil eye against the Good King Brendon.

On one such night, while the old hag stared into her filthy mirror, trying her best to convince herself she was all-powerful—using the hypnotic power of her evil eye— she placed a spell on herself unintentionally. The spell so paralyzed her that she could barely flip the patch down to stop the power of the stare. Hours passed as she gazed at her reflection in the mirror, her stringy hank of white hair, her grisly green face, and her one rotten tooth. She seemed nearly helpless. At last, with the greatest effort, Old Snag was able to flip the patch one last time, and she came to. Comforted by her pet snake, which draped over her shoulder, rats nibbling at her feet, she managed a sinister smile, revealing one ragged tooth.

The Heathen Banshee began to concoct a scheme to recapture the Magic Box by tricking her archenemy, the Good King Brendon. Flanked by the Thunder Lizard and her Fearless Vampire Bats, Snagnasty was convinced that with her superior shrewdness and the Magic Box, she could control the sun, the moon, the wind, and the earth itself to work her infamous black magic. Old Snag's wicked cackle terrified her snake and caused the rats to scurry to the shadows. Driven by revenge and hatred, she began to plot the details of a devious plan.

Coincidentally, on that very same night, the Good King Brendon's thoughts crept to Old Snag. He recalled the battle in which he subdued the Heathen Banshee, putting

a dagger into her eye. He remembered a horrendous life and death struggle between the forces of good and evil, the Heathen Banshee and her warriors having fought furiously. Before that battle, Old Snag had kidnapped many of the ancient gnome king's men and imprisoned them in her despicable dungeon. There they were thrown into a vat of boiling scum, which stripped them of their flesh and turned them into Sleeping Bones, skeletons that Old Snag was then able to control with her appalling powers. The Sleeping Bones became her warrior slaves, and they acted at her command, mindlessly.

The Heathen Banshee armed the zombie-like skeletons with swords and lances. They didn't need shields, since they had no flesh to stab, no blood to let, nothing to injure. Brendon and his warrior gnomes attacked with the broad side of their swords, using maces to smash the Sleeping Bones. He recalled the difficulty of driving the evil out of the land and across the Raging River to the Wild Lands, off into the cold and barren place known as Thunderlandia.

He could still hear the screaming and cursing of the Heathen Banshee as she retreated in pain after he mangled her eye. It made his blood run cold now, despite his roaring fire in the safe hearth of his home. The gnome king recalled Old Snag's army—broken, demoralized and defeated, scattering ahead as the Heathen Banshee followed them, her shame and pain thick as a river of blood. Brendon was certain that her wails that night could have wakened the dead.

After seizing the Magic Box, Brendon ordered his men to destroy Snagnasty's castle, stone by stone, so it could never be used for such wickedness again. Brendon also ordered all the creatures of the night to be chased from the land. Those demons, like the Heathen Banshee, then scattered to Thunderlandia.

To this day, the Good King Brendon was haunted by the specter of the Heathen Banshee. He knew she would never abandon her quest for the Magic Box. Because of this, the gnome king kept the whereabouts of the box a secret and used it very seldom. But on this night, warmed by his fire, he felt a terrible chill. He sensed the Heathen Banshee's treachery had reached a peak, and she would soon seek her revenge. The good king spent the rest of the night in a fit of worry. He knew his precious land would be destroyed if the Heathen Banshee should ever command the powers contained in the Magic Box.

It was an ordinary box, none too particular, none too pretty...

Chapter Two:

Once There Was a Gnome, an Evil Troll and a Silly Unicorn

Gnomes are known by various names. In some places they are called leprechauns, in others, gremlins or elves, or pixies (which they hate), or simply, little people. The Good King Brendon was king of all the gnomes, whatever their name. He ruled his kingdom with a firm, yet velvet hand, mixing wisdom and good grace with gentleness and integrity. Many of the gnomes he sent to far corners of the kingdom, where they were responsible for the land and the animals that lived there. They served the king and helped him to keep the land and its creatures safe and prosperous.

In the Good King Brendon's faraway land was one particular forest. The caretaker of that forest was a good, kind, and honest little gnome named Paddy Cornelius O'Shaughnessey. Paddy's forest area was a major part of the vast kingdom, which contained mighty trees and rolling hills, crystal clear lakes and streams. Paddy Cornelius O'Shaughnessey took great pride in the care of his king's ancient forest. He was proud that its woodlands were always green, lush and beautiful, that trees grew tall and sturdy, that the air smelled fresh, that the brooks and streams were clear and refreshing. But most important, Paddy was proud that all the forest creatures were happy and safe.

Gnomes, as we all know, possess a bit of magic. And to be sure, Paddy Cornelius O'Shaughnessey used this magic from time to time to make sure that everything was as it should be, while respecting that magic highly, and using it carefully. This impressed his king, for many gnomes were impetuous and used magic carelessly, sometimes causing more harm than good. Not so with Paddy Cornelius O'Shaughnessey. He preferred to work hard and not to rely on magic to complete his chores. Through the years, Paddy's love of hard work pleased his king very much—so much so, that Paddy became Brendon's favorite. As time passed, the Good King Brendon kept a watchful eye on his favorite gnome, for he knew someday that this special little fellow would be called upon for extraordinary deeds.

Every gnome wears a pointy red hat, a vest with many pockets (for a variety of tools) and a neat brown belt, smartly buckled over a soft cotton shirt. Wooden clogs keep their feet dry, while thick wool socks keep their toes warm. Gnomes sport long beards, which are red at first and turn silver with the advance of years. Paddy's beard was still bright red, for he was an Irish gnome. In fact, Paddy had known St. Patrick himself (who had the reddest of beards). Paddy Cornelius O'Shaughnessey had a twinkle in his eye, a smile on his lips and rosy red cheeks. When he stood up straight he was about as tall as a large man's hand; and if one were to stoop low enough, one couldn't help wondering at his deep green eyes. And if one stared into those eyes, he would swear he'd seen the face of God smiling back.

All gnomes are prone to be a bit melancholy. Such was the case with Paddy.

Sometimes at the end of an especially difficult day, he could be found sitting atop the rocky cliff that bordered the ancient forest, gazing westward at the majestic sea. At those times, Paddy took comfort in watching the sun fall into the sea. He would then turn and face eastward to watch the darkness gather around the treetops in his beloved forest. During these times, Paddy's heart ached with the loneliness he felt.

Most of the time his duties—which he performed so kindheartedly—consumed his days and nights and kept him busy. Often the little gnome would forget that he had no one to share his life. At other, sadder times, Paddy would distract himself by tending his roses. His rose garden gave him joy, even when he felt lonely. Over the years his garden increased in size, filling with beautiful red roses he called Love's Promise. The little gnome was humbled by their beauty and sweet fragrance. Other gnomes came from miles away in this faraway land to simply walk the narrow paths of Paddy's enchanting garden and marvel at its sights and smells. This attention filled Paddy with pride, though his heart was laced with sadness because there was no special someone to share the beauty of his wonderful rose garden.

The Good King Brendon knew these things about Paddy, knew his goodness, his gentleness and kindheartedness. He also knew of Paddy's bouts with melancholy, and he knew that if the Heathen Banshee ever returned to threaten his kingdom, he would call upon the little gnome he loved the most to save the day.

With the Heathen Banshee and all her wickedness in mind, the Good King Brendon sent a unicorn named Silverthorne into Paddy Cornelius O'Shaughnessey's

forest to take up residence. All gnomes have heard of unicorns, but as observant as a gnome is, not one had ever actually caught a glimpse of such a creature. Unicorns are very shy, and although they act silly at times, playing too long in the rain and splashing through mud puddles, they are careful to hide whenever anyone approaches. That includes even kind and gentle gnomes.

The very best thing about a unicorn—and this is why the king sent Silverthorne to Paddy—is that they bring good luck. Even though every gnome, including Paddy, had a bit of his own magic to use in protecting his forest region, the presence of a unicorn added a little more. In time, Paddy became aware of Silverthorne the Unicorn, although he could never ever see him, and it was a comfort to know the unicorn's luck was at hand. It was a comfort to Good King Brendon, too, since he suspected, as gnome kings do, that he might someday need the special magic of his beloved gnome and the sprightly unicorn.

Sure enough, one day darkness gathered in Paddy Cornelius O'Shaughnessey's forest. At the edge of his woods lay a particularly nasty spot. A dreary patch of land held a dingy, smelly hole in the ground where a vile creature lived: an evil troll. For some reason, every gnome had to protect his patch of forest from a troll's mischief.

Trolls were the sworn enemies of gnomes and busied themselves plotting harm and trouble. A troll is a nasty, ugly piece of work. All trolls, including Crag, have tiny red squinty eyes, since they don't like the cheery sunlight. They have noses like cucumbers, covered with pimples and warts. Their long noses are always running with snot and boogers until a hard, green, snot-caked crust makes breathing difficult. A trolls' mouth has ragged teeth and also smells horribly.

This Evil Troll Crag constantly scratched and muttered and complained. He believed that if he could capture and cage Paddy in his rotten little hole, he could then use the gnome's magic for his own evil ends.

The Evil Troll Crag wasn't a particularly skilled hunter and none too smart, so he resorted to eating what he could find, which were vulgar, slimy things, crawling in the dirt or in the mud at the bottom of swamps. All this made the troll a cranky sort, who grumbled and whined about how to make his miserable life a little bit better. One day while picking his toes, Crag hit on an idea about how to change his luck. It was simple—of course! The Evil Troll Crag was a simple sort. He would kidnap Silverthorne the Unicorn! Crag knew the gnome would try to rescue the unicorn. Crag could just hide and wait for the gnome, and then ambush him. With both a unicorn and a gnome as his captives, Crag's luck would surely change for the better.

It's a known fact that capturing a unicorn is nearly impossible, but as dumb luck would have it, the Evil Troll Crag accomplished it. Although Paddy was not aware of Silverthorne's capture, he immediately noticed, on one particular evening, while sitting on the rocks overlooking the majestic sea, that the stars didn't twinkle quite so brightly as usual. On his way home, Paddy noticed that the evening birds weren't singing as they nested in the giant oak trees. The streams didn't babble as cheerfully. The woods were not full of the usual chirping, chatter and general conversation. In

fact, everything seemed a bit forlorn, and as Paddy shivered with the unseasonable chill in the air, he knew something was terribly wrong. Instantly, the little gnome sensed the unicorn was in danger. The little gnome also knew at once that the Evil Troll Crag was behind it all. Paddy pledged then and there to save the unicorn, even if it meant entering the troll's stinking hole.

A troll is a nasty, ugly piece of work...

Chapter Three:

Once There Was a Unicorn in Distress – And a Worried Gnome

The Evil Troll Crag took no pleasure in anything he did. However, on capturing the unicorn, Crag actually giggled gleefully. He was sure his luck would change now, and for the better! After all, unicorns brought good luck, and capturing one would bring luck to the troll. And so it came to pass that Silverthorne the Unicorn was locked in a cage in the dank hole the Evil Troll Crag called home sweet home. All through the night the stupid troll watched Silverthorne through the bars of the cage, while the sad creature sang songs filled with despair. Outside the putrid hole the little gnome kept watch, listening with a broken heart, as the sad songs echoed his own melancholy. Paddy promised to rescue Silverthorne and make this faraway land a happy place again for both of them.

Besides being ugly, having bad breath, and having stinky armpits, a troll has a general body odor that would gag a maggot. Furthermore, a troll is always hungry. Those familiar with trolls know that their eating habits and customary diets are pitiful. Their diet of grubs, worms, slugs and slimly things living in mud puddles makes them temperamental. They get stomachaches, which foul their moods even more, and the

Evil Troll Crag had had his share. He hadn't caught many grubs for some time now, so his stomach rumbled, putting him in a nasty mood. Surely now he would find more grubs and wouldn't be so hungry. If he felt better, his own stinking odor wouldn't bother him so much. It was indeed a mystery how the Evil Troll Crag captured the unicorn, especially considering how elusive, secretive and shy they are.

Unicorns are playful, impetuous and silly. And although they are never seen—even by gnomes—their silliness sometimes causes them to make mistakes. Unlike gnomes, unicorns have no skills in magic; they just bring luck with them, wherever they go. Now the Evil Troll Crag was impatient for good luck to come his way. That dumb luck meant more food, a warmer fire, and plenty of creature comforts. He felt that his problems were solved, and it was time now to turn his attention to capturing and torturing Paddy Cornelius O'Shaughnessey. That was sure to bring still more luck, given the magic tendencies of a gnome. It was the best a miserable troll could hope for!

With Silverthorne the Unicorn safely tucked into a cage in his vile hole, the Evil Troll Crag sat down and picked his toes, then picked his nose and plotted a plan to capture the gnome. After a bit of thinking—if you can call it that—his head began to hurt.

Meanwhile, Paddy Cornelius O'Shaughnessey crept home and worried about Silverthorne. Sitting by a fire in his cozy living room, Paddy began to plan the unicorn's rescue. He then began to worry, as all gnomes do, about how his plan could work. Soon he drifted into melancholy, remembering hearing the unicorn's singing, deep in the forest after a spring rain. Paddy recalled with gratitude how Silverthorne's good luck had made the forest safer, and he wished again for those times.

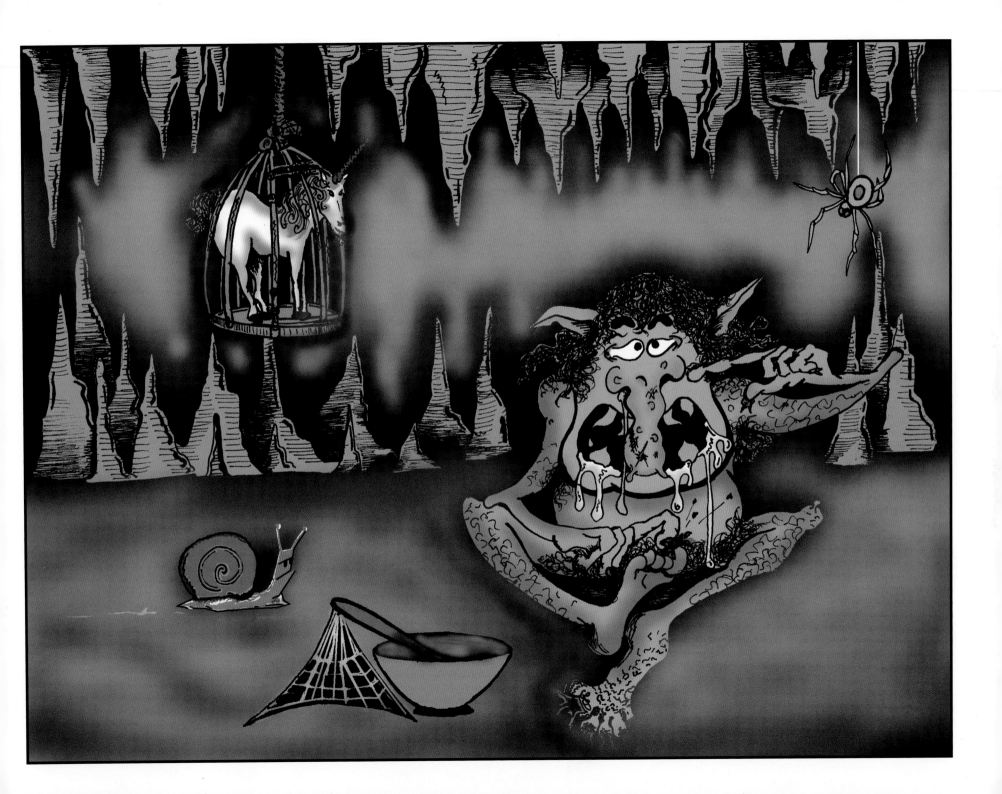

Chapter Four:

Once There Was Pumpkin…And Some Honey Bees

Suddenly summer wasn't summer anymore. The blueberries and blackberries crowded their bushes. The corn and pumpkins ripened in the field. The bees were busy with their last frantic attempts to collect honey from rapidly wilting flowers. Maple leaves were unseasonably red and yellow and already beginning to carpet the mossy forest floor. The afternoon shadows appeared earlier in the day and grew longer. There was a cool chill in the air. Paddy Cornelius O'Shaughnessey knew the reasons for these unexpected changes, and he also knew he couldn't stop them. Paddy's wonderful summer was slipping away into chilly autumn because the unicorn was not working his luck in the forest. Rescuing the unicorn was the only way to reverse the unexpected change of season.

Meanwhile the despicable troll threw more wood on his smoldering fire, filling his rank hole with black smoke, which choked both him and poor Silverthorne. When the smoke cleared, the troll settled into eyeballing the unicorn and waiting for his luck to change. In fact, that's all he did, day after day: he stared stupidly at the sad little unicorn with his red, pus-rimmed eyes. His luck wasn't changing, and he became more and more grumpy. Paddy Cornelius O'Shaughnessey, his stubby fingers holding his nose from the smell, would at times come close to the wicked troll's hole to spy on him. He had little hope of rescuing Silverthorne, since the Evil Troll Crag would never let the unicorn out of his sight. Paddy knew he must devise a trick to save the unicorn.

Whenever the gnome had a problem to solve, he found a quiet place to sit and think. His favorite place was his rose garden. To Paddy, that was the most peaceful spot on earth, and he'd stroll through the fragrant roses, letting his mind wander. He would then sit on an old stone in the middle of his roses, and before long a solution to his problems would come softly to mind. When pondering Silverthorne's dilemma, the first thing that came to mind was the change of the season, with images of pumpkins and bees!

Back in Crag's hole, the beast's stomach began to growl—a reminder that he was hungry, and that made him cranky. The troll's main weakness was food and not getting enough of it. Paddy Cornelius O'Shaughnessey could protect the forest and its creatures only by knowing the habits and weaknesses of the resident troll. In recent days he had been watching the troll and hearing his stomach grumble, and Paddy knew what he liked the best.

Even though it was still July, the air felt like October, and the fields were full of pumpkins. Paddy found the largest, juiciest pumpkin. He then went to work with knife and spoon to hollow it out. He then lugged it to a clearing in the woods by the old

swamp. Next, he hollowed out a few smaller pumpkins and took the guts and seeds and dropped them along the trail that led to the Evil Troll Crag's wretched hole.

After laying the first part of his trap, Paddy went to a beehive. Paddy Cornelius O'Shaughnessey didn't like to aggravate any forest creatures (most especially the bees) during sensitive times, which seemed, for bees, most of the time. However, in order to rescue Silverthorne, he had to resort to extreme measures: he must rouse the bees. Paddy quickly snatched a beehive from an alder tree and ran as fast as he could on his little clogs. Angry honeybees will sting even a gentle gnome. When he arrived at the hollowed out pumpkin in the clearing, he dropped the hive full of bees into it and quickly put the top back on. Voila!

The trap was set for the Evil Troll Crag. If all went according to plan, the troll would follow the trail of pumpkin seeds to the hollowed out pumpkin, open it up for a feast, and be surprised by angry bees.

Meanwhile, the troll moped miserably about his hole, studying the imprisoned unicorn and wondering when all this luck would find him. His patience was wearing thin, as his stomach growled. Soon he smelled the telltale aroma of pumpkins and decided to investigate. He stuck his cucumber nose outside his hole, sniffed the air, and saw a trail of pumpkin seeds and bits of pumpkin leading from his hole into the woods. Led by the promise of a succulent pumpkin feast, the troll stumbled through the thicket until he reached the clearing. There he discovered a sight for sore eyes: a giant pumpkin in all its radiant orange glory. He ran toward it as fast as his flat feet could carry him, smacking his lips, drooling sloppily, his large disgusting nose warty and pimply, oozing snot, yet smelling the sweetness of his favorite food. He heard a slight buzzing sound, but it could have been the ordinary ringing in his ears (it can happen when they are never cleaned).

When he reached the pumpkin, Crag realized it was too large to pick up for a big chomp. Yet, as luck would have it (at last the unicorn's luck was paying off!), he noticed the top was loose. He could lift off the top, which was just bite size. What a lucky day! The troll opened his mouth wide, his green teeth bared, and pulled off the top of the orange delight. As he did so, a thousand bees flew out, angry for being trapped inside a pumpkin. They began stinging Crag's head, his ears and his large grotesque nose.

Unfortunately, since Crag still had his mouth open, he caught a mouthful of furious bees and screamed in agony. With every yelp, a mouthful of bees swarmed out of Crag's crusty mouth. He then ran as fast as he could with a trail of angry bees swarming about his head, an occasional bee escaping his mouth when he screamed. Confused and in serious pain, the troll took off in the direction of the swamp, although he detested water. With the bees hovering and stinging, the miserable troll dived into the scummy swamp, leaving an oily slick on its muddy green surface.

During the Evil Troll Crag's miserable experience, Paddy Cornelius O'Shaughnessey slipped silently into the troll hole, loosened the latch of the cage that held the unicorn, and set Silverthorne free! The unicorn giggled, bucked and reared on his tiny back legs and pranced off into the woods, delighted at his new freedom.

Paddy couldn't resist returning to the clearing to see what had become of Crag. A sly smile crossed his face as he saw the unlucky troll blubbering, howling and splashing in the grimy swamp, thousands of agitated honeybees still hovering above him.

Eventually, the bees gave up and flew off to build a new hive. The Evil Troll Crag, stung and bitten, tired and nearly drowned, but mostly angry and still hungry, dolefully shuffled back to his cave. When he arrived at his cave he saw the unicorn was gone as well. Not only would Crag have no more good luck, he'd had an overdose of bad.

Worse, the Evil Troll Crag knew that he had been tricked, tortured and forced to jump into a swamp by a mere gnome. Looking over his hairy shoulder and smelling of the foul swamp, Crag spied Paddy trotting through the woods, his wooden clogs clicking on the tree roots and branches of the forest floor. As Paddy scampered out of sight, the troll screamed: "I'll get you, Paddy Cornelius O'Shaughnessey! I'll get you if it's the last thing I do!"

To make matters worse, the filthy troll heard a chuckle coming from the thicket nearby. Crag recognized the sound from recent days and knew that now familiar laugh. It was Silverthorne the Unicorn. Crag flopped down next to the smoldering fire in his stinky cave and began to whimper wretchedly.

Chapter Five:

Once There Was an Evil Hawk

Once the kidnapping caper was put to rest, tranquility was restored to the ancient forest, and a comfortable, quiet routine returned. That is, until the day the Evil Hawk soared above the trees. This fearsome predator glided through the air and with its terrible eyes surveyed the woodland creatures—especially the bite-sized ones, like the squirrels, the rabbits and the chipmunks. There was plenty of food for a hawk in Paddy's woods. The hawk returned often to hunt and to terrorize. Soon the forest creatures lived in a constant state of fear. The spirit of the forest darkened. This was now a dangerous place, and the gnome was unable to protect his friends. Like the other forest creatures, he felt helpless and was tormented day and night by the hawk.

Even though a gnome can work magic, and his responsibility is to protect those who depend upon him, he cannot harm another creature while doing so. Thus, Paddy could not use magic against the hawk, because the great bird was one of nature's creatures. Paddy was at a loss as to what to do.

To make matters worse, the Evil Troll Crag held a grudge about losing the unicorn and was continually up to no good. This time his plan was to capture the hawk. Even though his logic was twisted and harebrained, the troll reasoned that he could use the hawk, which dominated the sky, to prey on small woodland creatures. That way Crag could expand his menu from grubs to more delectable treats, like chipmunks. Perhaps he could even use the hawk to nab Paddy Cornelius O'Shaughnessey. Gathering what few wits he had, the Evil Troll Crag set a trap and, much to his surprise and wicked delight, captured the hawk. But hanging onto a captive hawk was another thing altogether. Being a truly cunning and dangerous creature, the hawk escaped by wounding the troll with his razor sharp talons and vicious beak. During the struggle, however, the troll managed to do some damage. He damaged one of the Evil Hawk's wings—so much so, that the bird was left to stalk the earth, dragging his injured wing worthlessly by his side.

Although the woodland creatures knew the hawk had lost much of his menace and could no longer dominate the sky, they were still fearful. Even the more daring animals—the foxes, coyotes, weasels and stoats—soon discovered that there was easier prey elsewhere, prey without talons and a cruel beak. Yet the Evil Hawk remained miserable.

What the other animals didn't know was that the hawk was also very much afraid, especially at night. No longer able to escape into the sky, the hawk now feared the sounds that were more ominous and threatening on the forest floor after dark. And

like every other small creature scratching the earth for food, the hawk was wary of the shadows and whatever lurked there. Before long, as other creatures had before him, the hawk came finally to Paddy Cornelius O'Shaughnessey to ask for his help.

Yet each time the hawk dragged himself and his wing to Paddy, he was rejected. All Paddy could do was feed the great bird. He could not use magic to adjust natural laws. That is, he could not restore the hawk's damaged wing. After several visits to him, the hawk sadly returned to the gnome, asking for death. This request alarmed Paddy. He explained to the hawk that he could not grant such a wish either, for a gnome can do no harm. It is against his nature. Alas, the proud bird would not accept this answer. Again and again, he begged the gnome.

Eventually his pleading wore Paddy down, and the gnome agreed to magically heal the shattered wing. Still, the humble gnome was consumed with worry about using magic for unnatural action. All injured beasts must face nature's fate. Although a gnome could rescue animals in distress and do many good deeds that benefited the forest and its creatures, altering the course of nature with magic was just wrong. As Paddy worried, he nevertheless repaired the broken wing. He miraculously healed and strengthened the bird. His health restored, the grateful hawk promised to leave, never to return to Paddy's forest again. Before his departure, the once Evil Hawk pledged eternal friendship to Paddy and promised the gnome that he would someday return the gnome's kind favor.

Paddy, ever humble, asked only for the hawk's friendship in return. And so, the once Evil Hawk, now hale and strong of wing, his confidence restored, bid Paddy

farewell. Paddy blinked back a tear as he watched the hawk fly away, above the forest and away toward Thunderlandia. The little gnome hoped with all his heart that the wind would always be under his wings, bearing him where the sun sails and the moon walks. Paddy watched the beautiful, noble bird effortlessly pass over ancient oak trees. The little person with the pointy red hat took a deep breath of crisp morning air and cracked a smile. Even though there was a mist in the hollows that chilled the forest, it was once again a good place to be. From the majestic sea to the pinnacles of the tallest trees, peace was restored to Paddy's land. Paddy ambled contentedly through his beloved rose garden, sniffing its perfumes, his faith in nature renewed. He was eager to do more good deeds. The gnome took one last glance at the sky and saw the hawk slowly disappear on the horizon. Paddy then whispered after his newfound friend: "Peace B'darvey."

Chapter Six:

Once There Was a Visit from the Good King Brendon

1nevitably, another shadow drifted upon Paddy Cornelius O'Shaughnessey's ancient forest. This shroud was similar to the capture of Silverthorne the Unicorn. Again it was late summer, when the leaves started to fall, the flowers bent their heads, and the winds began to bluster across the meadows. This time Paddy knew black magic was lurking. He felt it in his heart and feared this strange and sudden darkness would not soon disappear. Angry gray clouds covered the sun, which caused even the shy and peaceful forest creatures to become cantankerous.

On one miserable day, while Paddy Cornelius O'Shaughnessey was bustling about his humble home, he heard a step on his stoop and a quiet rap at the door. It gave him a fright, for he expected no visitors. All forest gnomes live beneath sturdy oaks in tiny homes in the tree roots. Gnomes are secretive about where they live, and most forest animals have no idea where to find them. These little people are private about their homes and families. So Paddy opened the door carefully. He jumped in surprise at seeing the Good King Brendon huddled on his doorstep in a heavy winter cloak. It was summer, yet Paddy noticed his king's breath in the chilly air.

It was a great honor to have the gnome king visit. Such visits were rare and usually accompanied by much pomp and circumstance. They occurred after some great achievement, above and beyond a gnome's normal duties. Paddy was perplexed, to say the least. Paddy knew he had not distinguished himself in a way that would bring the king of all the gnomes to his home, and he noticed the grim expression on the Good King Brendon's face, minus the twinkle in his usually smiling eyes. In fact, all the little gnome saw in those eyes was sadness and despair. A dutiful gnome, Paddy made his king welcome, offering him a chair by the roaring fire and good food and drink.

Paddy then prepared himself, knowing that his king's grief had something to do with the wickedness in this ancient land. Having enjoyed a good meal and the warm hospitality of his host, the royal guest lit his pipe and leaned back in Paddy's great chair with a deep sigh. The Good King Brendon closed his weary eyes as tendrils of pipe smoke filled the air of Paddy's sitting room. They both sat quietly. Soon the king opened his eyes and began telling Paddy solemnly that this beloved land was in grave danger. The Heathen Banshee had stolen the Magic Box and was plotting black magic.

The Good King Brendon had heard rumors that Old Snag had the box hidden away in her lair beneath Thunder Mountain, where it lay under the watchful eyes of the Two-Headed Thunder Lizard. Worst still, the gnome king was powerless to retrieve the Magic Box. He had come to Paddy Cornelius O'Shaughnessey to ask a special favor. Would Paddy journey across the Raging River and through the Wild Lands into Thunderlandia to retrieve the Magic Box?

Paddy Cornelius O'Shaughnessey was flabbergasted! Most gnomes are timid, and Paddy was without a doubt the shyest and most bashful gnome that lived. There were times when he was afraid of his own shadow.

Paddy protested to his king, "But such a quest, such a responsibility, is far beyond my ability! And my good king, I am hardly worthy, being neither strong nor brave!"

Paddy was pacing around the room, his hands rubbing his arms, his face anxious. He continued as the king listened silently.

"I tend roses! I am a humble guardian of this ancient forest. My dear king, I am not a warrior gnome."

The Good King Brendon smiled a sad smile at Paddy. His tone was gentle.

"Yes, Paddy I hold your goodness, honesty and kindness in high esteem. There is great power in those qualities, and they will serve you well in overcoming any evil that may befall you on your journey to Thunderlandia."

Paddy implored his king to reconsider, wondering who would tend his forest, now that things were so unsettled? Besides, Paddy didn't even know how to use a weapon; he never had owned one. Not even a slingshot. He was afraid of them.

The good king quieted his friend, saying, "You will not need a weapon, Paddy. You'll be protected by your goodness, honesty, and kindness. Those attributes, which you hold fast to each day, will provide all the strength and courage you will need, to face the evil in Thunderlandia."

"Those qualities, in fact, allowed you to tame the Evil Hawk, befriend an elusive unicorn and save them both from terrible fates," said the king. "Those qualities will aid you in your journey, Paddy."

The gnome king assured Paddy that the unicorn would accompany him on his quest and that they would become reliable, trusted friends. With Paddy's magic and Silverthorne's luck there would be enough power, strength and courage to overcome any evil the Heathen Banshee dared throw in their path. Furthermore, because Paddy was an excellent woodsman, the forest itself, even the feared Wild Lands, would offer adequate protection in times of danger.

None of the king's kind and encouraging words gave Paddy any comfort. He was more frightened than ever. In a weak, trembling voice Paddy reminded his king, "In the Wild Lands there are not only evil trolls but also Terrible Orcs and other mongrel beasts! The Two-Headed Thunder Lizard lives beneath Thunder Mountain and all the entrances are guarded by the Fearless Vampire Bats! Even if I could get that far, I would still have to get past the Wicked Lizard Wizard. I have no sword, no shield, and I wouldn't know how to use them anyway! Goodness and kindness are no weapons against such savages. Honesty will not protect me against vile things wishing to do me harm." Then the little gnome hung his head, ashamed of his own fear and cowardice.

Once again the good king smiled at Paddy, sadly shaking his head, his long beard swaying back and forth, and said: "Paddy, Paddy, your honesty and goodness and kindness are strong weapons, and they will indeed protect you. Your magic is strong enough. The creatures you will encounter are not totally evil; they are miserable, and

their misery comes from their mean spiritedness. They can be tricked, just as you tricked the troll. Even the Wicked Lizard Wizard can be beaten. The Fearless Vampire Bats can also be subdued. And I have something else that can help you."

The Good King Brendon then pulled a little wooden box out of the pocket of his great coat. He opened it and produced a perfect little shamrock. Its four leaves seemed to glow a brilliant green. Paddy couldn't believe its beauty. Indeed, he felt a certain strength and a bit of courage just gazing at its shining light.

"Paddy, take this with you", said the king.

Paddy retorted, "But it's only a shamrock!"

The king replied: "Yes, Paddy Cornelius O'Shaughnessey, but this one has four leaves, rather than three. This shamrock has special power. You of all people should be

"This shamrock has special power...Keep the shamrock close; cherish its strength, for it is a sacred treasure..."

acquainted with the power of the shamrock. Remember when you once helped St. Patrick use its magic to drive the snakes from that emerald island? Well, this shamrock will be your protection. For you alone I added the fourth leaf, for further protection. This provides all you need beyond your character and the company of the unicorn. Keep the shamrock close; cherish its strength, for it is a sacred treasure. This one comes from the holy ground in Phoenix Park."

Paddy, ever reluctant, desperately begged the good king to reconsider. He had only encountered the unicorn once. He beseeched his king to understand that a unicorn is shy and silly, not a reliable creature to bring into battle. And besides, he asked, "What are the chances of ever finding that elusive unicorn again?"

The king smiled and said, "All you have to do is call for him, and he will come to your side. Go into the clearing amid the giant evergreens when the night is at its most quiet. Just call him."

The Good King Brendon slowly rose from his chair. "I'm departing now Paddy. It is also time for you to go. Your journey must begin immediately. There is no time to waste. Trust the power and magic of the shamrock; it will serve you well when used wisely." He paused and searched Paddy's eyes for acceptance. He added, "Remember your goodness always, your kindness, your honesty, and your love for all living things. They will strengthen you and give you courage."

He then turned to the doorway, paused and turned back to Paddy to say firmly, "Don't forget Paddy: you can only use the shamrock's power once, and then only

when all else fails! The mystical power of the shamrock, blessed by our greatest holy man St. Patrick himself, can strike terror into the most fearsome beast, even the Heathen Banshee herself." He tapped the tobacco out of his pipe and muttered, "Be mindful to use the song of the unicorn. Take your harp and play your songs to accompany him when he sings his songs. Though they are sad, they lift the spirit and offer protection during the dark times you are sure to encounter." There was a prolonged silence while Paddy stared at his feet, snug in his woolen socks.

The king continued softly, "As you journey through the Wild Lands and into Thunderlandia, keep the shamrock over your heart and use it wisely. It will protect the good and honest, while the evil will shy away from its brilliance. Remember Paddy, there are four leaves on this shamrock: one is for hope, for you must never give up. One is for faith, which you must never forsake. One is for love, because we cannot live without it, and the last I give to you for a bit of extra luck."

Paddy then reached for the door but was stopped by the warm hand of his king on his shoulder. "Paddy, one more thing before you begin your quest. Once you have the Magic Box—and I'm confident you will return it safely—resist any temptation you may have to open it and peer inside. The mysteries of the box are tempting. Once the power of the box is unleashed, it will be impossible to control. The Heathen Banshee knows this, now that she has the box. One of the reasons the darkness in the forest is not more dismal is because the hag hasn't learned to control the power of the box. Promise me, Paddy Cornelius O'Shaughnessey, that you will use your whole mind, your full will and your entire strength to resist the power of the Magic Box."

Paddy had only been in the company of his king during times of celebration. He had never seen him so grim. Paddy looked into Brendon's green eyes, which had always gleamed like sunshine before but were now like a cloudy pool, and replied in barely a whisper: "I promise, my king."

The king whispered in reply: "Then be off, my son, and Peace B'darvey."

That same evening in the clearing in the middle of Paddy's beloved ancient forest he called to the unicorn. Silverthorne came instantly, as if on a gentle wind. Without question or reservation the shy unicorn agreed to accompany Paddy on this most dangerous journey. Distressed that the Heathen Banshee had stolen the Magic Box and brought such darkness to this wonderful land, Silverthorne longed to celebrate the glory of rainbows again.

Paddy and Silverthorne stood together in a forest clearing under the silver moon. In the chill, they began to shiver. Was it from the cold or the unknown they faced? Paddy, armed with his goodness, kindness and honesty, as well as the shamrock, thought of his king near the fire, smoke from his magnificent pipe filling the room. He thought of the haunted expression on his king's gentle face and shivered. The Good King Brendon and all his subjects depended on him; he must not fail. Paddy searched for some comfort in his king's parting works, "Peace B'darvey". It is an Irish leprechaun phrase for "welcome" or "goodbye," and it means "best wishes," "good luck always," and "peace be with you." It was time to go.

And so the newfound friends began their quest, first stopping at the roots of the oak to secure Paddy's cottage and to pack the precious harp. Paddy hoped that somewhere soon he could strum his harp while Silverthorne sang beautiful songs, soothing souls, warming hearts and keeping all danger at bay.

The newfound friends began their quest, first stopping at the roots of the oak to secure Paddy's cottage and to pack the precious harp...

44

Chapter Seven

Once There Were Two Pesky Polecats and an Evil Troll

Paddy Cornelius O'Shaughnessey was painfully aware that the way to Thunderlandia would not be easy. Even the beginning would prove a challenge. In order to leave the peaceful, faraway land of the Good King Brendon, the two adventurers had to first cross the Raging River by way of an old stone bridge. Approaching the stone bridge they discovered the Evil Troll Crag lying in wait under it, hoping for some unsuspecting critter to serve as an easy meal.

Since this was the only passage between the two lands, and since the only creatures ever to use the bridge were desperate to escape the terrors of the Wild Lands, the Evil Troll Crag expected to have easy pickings. There he sat on his hairy haunches in the murky darkness, hidden in the chill shadows of the bridge—rubbing his watery, pus-rimmed red eyes, his nose clogged with crusty and slimy snot, his green teeth slimy with slobber and drool, smacking his crusty lips. Although Crag thought himself quite the clever fellow in his hiding place, with his stomach constantly rumbling, he wasn't hiding well or fooling anyone.

The good luck of the unicorn paid off quickly in sniffing out the troll. Paddy, always in a mood to aggravate the troll, concocted a plan to flush out the cunning beast so that he and the unicorn could scamper across the bridge unharmed to begin their real adventure.

Down a nearby path was a foul swamp. It was the same disgusting pond where the Evil Troll Crag sought refuge from the angry bees. It was also home to two ornery, mangy polecats. These two polecats caused poor Paddy nothing but trouble with their obnoxious pranks, which upset the peace and tranquility of the ancient forest. They were much like the Evil Troll Crag, except they weren't as nasty. They were simply a nuisance. They ate most anything they found, bugs, slugs and whatever they could scrounge from the bottom of the swamp. Like the troll, they were always hungry. Paddy knew the polecats enjoyed nothing more than playing tricks on Crag and stealing his grubs.

Paddy had learned that the two polecats were fearless creatures. Their behavior was so obnoxious that the rest of the forest creatures, even the coyotes and foxes, left them alone. As a result nothing in the forest posed a danger to the polecats, especially the Evil Troll Crag. In fact, whenever the two tricksters felt inclined, they would mercilessly tease the troll, dash into their swamp, splash around in the muck and then hide. All the while the troll would stand on the muddy shore, out of breath from chasing them, cursing them. The polecats knew he despised water of any kind, especially the foul, polluted swamp water, and would never follow them into the swamp.

While the Evil Troll Crag thought he was cleverly hidden under the stone bridge, Paddy and Silverthorne snuck back to his fetid hole and, holding their breath to prevent inhaling the stench, slipped inside and grabbed a bucket of grubs, worms and slugs the troll was (no doubt) saving for dinner. The troll had evidently kept a batch of his usual food handy, in case he had no luck at the old bridge. Paddy and the unicorn found a spot between the old bridge and the murky swamp and began to drop the troll's precious food on the ground, making a trail from the swamp to the bridge. Before long, the ornery polecats and the Evil Troll Crag would smell the grubs and come to investigate.

Their trap set, the gnome and the unicorn scampered to a hillock above the Raging River to wait and watch. Soon enough, the revolting troll stuck his ugly head out from under the stone bridge and sniffed the air. His cucumber nose (warts, bee stings and all) savored the smell of grubs, and his mouth began to water. Further down the trail, the pesky polecats clambered out of the swamp water, scuffling and tussling with one another, covered with filth and mud. They sniffed and were drawn by the delectable smell of those grubs as well, and their mouths, too, began to water.

The Evil Troll Crag trundled out from under the bridge and fumbled along the riverside until he located the source of the smell. He picked up his favorite food with his grubby fingers, slurping loudly, much as he did with the pumpkin, following the trail laid out for him by the two tricksters. Paddy chuckled at how easily Crag could be fooled by such a simple plan.

Paddy spied the polecats nibbling and munching on the grubs, chattering along a collision course with the troll. Soon the only thing between the troll and the two pesky varmints was a stand of willow trees. Crag then rounded the willows and saw a bucket! It looked oddly familiar. He realized in a flash that the grubs he had been slurping had also been his. He had saved them in case his ambush didn't work. By then, the dimwitted troll understood that there was some treachery involved, and his face turned red with anger. Before the troll could decide what to do, from around the other side of the stand of willows appeared the two ornery polecats, smacking their lips and laughing at their good fortune in finding delicacies at their feet. The troll knew the swamp rats were notorious tricksters and immediately thought they had stolen his grubs. Fuming, and collecting all the meanness he could muster, the troll let out a blood-curdling wail and charged at the polecats.

The thing about polecats is that they're quick on their feet. Both started running circles around the clumsy troll, snorting and poking fun at him. What a hoot: another chance to tease the miserable troll. During the fracas and confusion, all three bumped and thumped into each other, falling into a smelly, furry heap on the ground. The troll struggled to jump up first, snarling, baring his ugly green fangs. All this unexpected activity caused the troll's crusty skin to itch. While the distracted troll slobbered and scratched at himself, the polecats raced away to their swamp. Crag was soon at their heels, snatching at them, growling and loudly snarling.

With all this disturbance in the forest, Paddy Cornelius O'Shaughnessey and

Silverthorne the Unicorn shot from their vantage point down the little hill and ran through the thicket to the old stone bridge. As the Evil Troll Crag and the two mangy polecats disappeared into the distance, the two friends clattered across the old stone bridge into the Wild Lands. They soon found the path to Thunderlandia.

The adventurers glimpsed where the mangy polecats were leading Crag, and wild with laughter, the polecats soon plunged into the muddy swamp. Along stumbled the Evil Troll Crag in pursuit, his big, clumsy feet tripping over one another, undone as he was. Finally the troll careened out of control at the edge of the swamp, grabbed an alder branch from a small tree and snapped it off as he fell head first into the green muck. KERPLUNK!

The next thing Paddy and Silverthorne saw was the troll's pink head bobbing to the top of the swamp. They heard him screaming and hollering at his misfortune, snot scumming from his nose, his beady red eyes glistening in the sunlight. With the Evil Troll Crag's shrieks echoing in the forest, and their troll troubles behind them, the two travelers pushed toward their next adventure. Paddy touched his breast to feel the shamrock and, reassured, trudged toward his destiny. Despite the apprehension they felt about their upcoming adventure, a tiny smile crossed Paddy's lips for having once again tricked the dastardly Crag. It was a satisfying achievement.

Chapter Eight

Once There Were Terrible Orcs

Along the road to Thunderlandia a traveler first encountered the Wild Lands. That grim place was a forsaken land of dark woods and swamps teeming with creepy, crawly, slimy creatures. The narrow path Paddy and Silverthorne had to follow crossed those swamps and came close to dank caves that smelled of dead and rotting things, and forced them to splatter through puddles of oozing goo. Shadows seemed to move in every direction. Emerging from those shadows were snakes, toads, lizards—all scary with their tiny eyes glowing in the darkness, whether night or day. For even the days were dark and dreary in the Wild Lands.

If that wasn't bad enough, Paddy and Silverthorne suffered the constant drizzle of black rain and thick fog in the Wild Lands. The sun was merely a faint, faraway haze in the sky. While tramping through this miserable darkness, creepy crawlies slimed and slithered at the feet and hooves of the two travelers. Occasionally some unknown thing snagged an ankle, causing one of them to jump or yelp.

The little gnome and the shy unicorn were in constant fear as they made their way through the Wild Lands. They tried to keep their spirits up, Paddy reassuring himself

with the sage words of Good King Brendon. At times, Paddy played his harp, while Silverthorne sang. If there were any evil or troubled souls lurking in the darkness (most certainly there were), the travelers hoped to soften those cold hearts by making them warm with their music, thus keeping danger at bay.

As frightening as all this proved to be, Paddy and Silverthorne knew that the Wild Lands' most fearsome creatures were the Terrible Orcs, which they had not encountered—yet! Certainly, the worst was still to come. On the very first night as the two friends crested a hill at the edge of some mangled trees not far from the swampland, they saw ahead of them a pack of Terrible Orcs. The orcs were huddled around a campfire, eating their customary meal of bug stew and worm soup. Paddy could smell the pot bubbling, its putrid fumes carried on the wind. It made his already queasy stomach turn.

Terrible Orcs are hairless creatures with warts and scabs covering their round, bald heads. Like trolls, orcs have small, beady red eyes. They have large bulbous noses, big floppy green lips and filthy brown teeth. What they were best known for, however, is the odor coming from their back ends. The orcs' backsides were forever roaring with gas because of the wretched food they ate. The smell was a good thing, since it served as warning that orcs lurked about. If that weren't bad enough, the front end was repulsive as well. Terrible Orcs' breath stunk like the inside of an old boot left in a mud puddle too long. There is no point mentioning the toe jam between their gnarly toes and the crusty clumps of earwax plugging their piggish ears. Another good thing about orcs was that sunlight stung their squinty red eyes (when it occasionally shone in the Wild Lands), so they came out only after dark. Paddy and Silverthorne knew they didn't have to worry about the Terrible Orcs in the daytime and guessed that their horrible smell would warn them in any case. It was always smart to keep a healthy distance from the Terrible Orcs, because if they got their grisly hands on a gnome or a unicorn, there was no telling what harm would ensue.

The smell became more and more unbearable, the closer our heroes came. Weary and bone tired as the two travelers were, they decided to go further on the treacherous trail, camping as far from the Terrible Orcs as possible. They couldn't risk one of the orcs stumbling across a slumbering gnome or unicorn while they slept! First they must sneak past the beasts' camp, since there was only one trail through the surrounding woods. It was dangerous there, particularly at night. Although Terrible Orcs have poor eyesight, their sense of smell and hearing are excellent, so they know when other creatures are near. Sneaking past the orcs was risky indeed!

This time Silverthorne had an idea, and he sprang into action, with no warning to Paddy. The gnome gasped as the little unicorn pranced boldly up to the camp, intentionally catching the attention of the smelly creatures. As one might expect, the Terrible Orcs all jumped as soon as their noses sniffed the unicorn. He would do in the stew! they growled. Silverthorne began to glow fiercely in the darkness. He grew brighter and brighter, and the unexpected light in the dark woods stung the eyes of the foul smelling brutes, bringing burning tears. With the orcs thus distracted, Paddy pulled out his precious harp and began to pluck the strings. Silverthorne then began

to sing melancholy songs. Soon the terrible orcs became drowsy, and, one by one, fell into deep slumber. While the creatures snored, their bottoms now and then emitted foul gas after their dreadful meal, and our two heroes slogged safely through the camp. Once they passed them, Paddy stole one last glance at the pack of nasty orcs, oblivious now to everything. He saw flies crawling on their snoring lips and shuddered.

Later that night, having found a safe place to camp, Paddy brought out his harp and filled the darkness with song. The unicorn soon began to sing too, and together they created enchanting music never before heard in that distressed land. To their surprise, bullfrogs in a nearby swamp belching their peculiar, unsettling calls, joined them. It was a strange and wonderful moment. And for a little while the Wild Lands were quiet and peaceful.

Chapter Nine:

Once There Were Almost Hot Buttered Babies

With one more strange adventure safely behind them, the two friends trekked bravely into the darkness, slowly approaching Thunderlandia. They marveled at how simple it had been to escape the clutches of the Terrible Orcs. Yet they were wary of the dangers that lurked around the next bend in their path. Nightmares like the Fearless Vampire Bats, a Two-Headed Thunder Lizard and of course, Old Snag, the Heathen Banshee, remained. Worse yet, somewhere amid the mountain rocks and dead spaces ahead crouched the Wicked Wizard Lizard and his bloodthirsty henchman, the Snafferjabber. Indeed, while Paddy and his unicorn worried, their approach was duly noted. As the gnome and the unicorn drew closer to its lookout among the jagged rocks, watching and waiting was the Snafferjabber, tittering to itself at its newly found prey.

The Snafferjabber was a sorry creature. At first glance it looked like an alligator standing hunch-backed on its two rear stick-like legs. It balanced itself using a wide tail that swished back and forth menacingly. Its tail had wart-like bumps down the middle and two spikes on the very end. This Snafferjabber had claws on both hands which were once sharp but were now chipped and jagged. On its head were patches of scraggly hair. Bugs crawled around open sores in the bald spots where the hair long ago refused to grow. The disgusting creature constantly scratched and dug at the sores on its head to chase away the bugs. Sharp, crooked fangs poked out every which way from its wide, sloppy mouth.

The Snafferjabber was the sidekick of the Wicked Wizard Lizard, and of these two pitiful renegades, the Wicked Wizard Lizard was definitely the brains of the operation. He called the shots, while the Snafferjabber did the dirty work, which in this case would be catching the gnome and the unicorn, cooking them and serving them up, hot and buttered. As pathetic as it was, the Snafferjabber still managed to look menacing as it eyeballed the two adventurers, smacking its ugly, scabby lips, muttering "hot buttered babies!"

In fact, that is all the beast exclaimed, again and again, all the while hoping to fry poor Paddy and Silverthorne in a buttery sauce over an open fire. In anticipation of this thrilling feast, the Snafferjabber began to drool a peculiar slime, which dripped from its ugly mouth. The creature's yellow eyes grew misty with expectation of a decent meal for a change. The Snafferjabber was tired of gagging on crusty scruds and rock cooties every breakfast, lunch and dinner.

"Be patient my pet," warned the Wicked Wizard Lizard in a whisper, startling the Snafferjabber out of its reverie.

Having seen his sidekick in action time and again, the wizard knew the Snafferjabber acted without thinking and often ruined their most careful schemes. Indeed, the wizard himself knew all too well the problems brought by acting impulsively. The Wicked Wizard Lizard had once been an advisor to an ancient king. He was a valued member of the king's court and lived in high style in the castle. He wore long, beautiful robes adorned with gold, diamonds and rubies, and he wore emerald rings on his fingers.

However, the Wicked Wizard Lizard had a dark heart and spent much of his time in the castle's dank cellar concocting potions and evil spells. He plotted to rob his king of all power and happiness. He used rats, bats, salamanders, snakes and tails of this, and eyeballs of that, and whatever else he could catch to throw into his pot, boiling it until the seedy mix took on a life of its own. With this potion, he conjured evil. Eventually, all of his tricks and treachery backfired, due to poor planning and impulsive behavior. Before long, the wizard's treachery was discovered, and he was banished to the jagged rocky mountains west of Thunderlandia, reducing him to bitterness and loathing, rendering his magic worthless. But now he, too, lay in wait alongside his lackey, the Snafferjabber, eyeballing Paddy Cornelius O'Shaughnessey and Silverthorne the Unicorn.

The rocky Wild Lands, which were home to the Snafferjabber and the Wicked Wizard Lizard, were separated from Thunderlandia by a dangerous river with treacherous currents. The only way across this river was over a precarious rope bridge strung

over a giant waterfall. The Snafferjabber stood constant guard at the bridge in hopes of snagging an unsuspecting critter for a good meal, since it was tired of gagging on crusted scruds and rock cooties three times a day.

When the gnome and the unicorn arrived at the rope bridge, they worried about crossing. Rumors of the Wicked Wizard Lizard suggested that he and his hideous sidekick hid nearby, perhaps watching the bridge to ambush them as they crossed the perilous rope bridge. Nonetheless, Paddy took a deep breath, patted the shamrock at his breast for courage, touched the unicorn's horn for luck, and with Silverthorne, ventured tentatively across the swaying bridge, the spray and mist from the waterfall complicating their dangerous passage.

The rope bridge was suspended at a dizzying height above the waterfall. The few who dared to cross never looked down, lest they lose courage. The gnome and the unicorn had made it halfway across, when suddenly the bridge began to swing and sway under them! As if crossing the rope bridge was not ordeal enough, they looked up and saw ahead of them the two most hideous creatures they had ever laid eyes on, running crazily toward them! They were fiercer by far than the Evil Troll Crag. Immediately Paddy and Silverthorne turned and began sprinting back the way they had come, the two demons fast at their heels. The Snafferjabber screamed, "Hot buttered babies, hot buttered babies!" Its long tongue licked at its lips, spit spraying from its grimy mouth.

The unicorn ran faster than the gnome and escaped the wizard and his henchman, scampering to safety. Paddy however, was trapped on the bridge, staring into two sets of unsettling yellow eyes; one was the Snafferjabber and the other the Wicked Wizard Lizard, craven beasts if ever there were any. Paddy was convinced then and there that all the rumors were true about the Wicked Wizard Lizard having no heart or soul. The scummy henchman constantly screeched, "Hot buttered babies! Real Babies! Tasty babies! Yummy, yummy in my tummy babies! No rock cooties tonight!"

From the Snafferjabber came a cackling, raspy laugh which became a revolting cough. Despite his terror, Paddy was afraid he would be sick to his stomach, so disturbing was the sound. Suddenly the Snafferjabber lashed at him. The gnome ducked, but the beast's long, jagged claw snagged the back of Paddy's belt and began to drag him along the bridge. The commotion caused the slippery rope bridge to sway out of control, and stirred panic in both of them, swaying at such a dizzying height. Below them lay sharp rocks and swirling water for what seemed a mile down. To fall meant certain death.

From the relative safety of his hiding place among the rocks, the unicorn watched in horror at his friend's peril. Disregarding his own life, he galloped back onto the slick rope bridge and butted the Snafferjabber in the behind with his horn. The beast screamed in pain, flinging its arms up to catch its balance, and lost its grip on the little gnome. That action threw Paddy Cornelius O'Shaughnessey into the air and over the ropes of the bridge. Down and down he fell. Paddy's life flashed before him as he sailed downward, picking up speed as he drifted helplessly toward the rocks and the turbulent water below—and certain death!

Silverthorne scrambled off the bridge toward Thunderlandia and back to safety in the confusion. The Wicked Wizard Lizard and the Snafferjabber were grabbing at each other and clutched the ropes for dear life, as the bridge shook out of control. Silverthorne watched helplessly as Paddy tumbled closer to the jagged rocks below. In a flash, just as Paddy prepared for death, out of nowhere appeared a hawk. This was not just any hawk, but the once Evil Hawk who had hunted Paddy's ancient forest in search of prey. As Paddy descended into the spray of the roaring waterfall and his fate below, the once Evil Hawk dove down toward the turbulent water as fast as he could fly. The great bird was moving at full speed in pursuit of the gnome. He had never flown faster. The muscles and tendons in his wings were strained, and his injured wing, though repaired by Paddy's magic, gave him excruciating pain as its strength was tested.

Both Paddy and the hawk shot straight into the spray at the rocky foot of the great waterfall. The roar of the water was deafening. Silverthorne could see nothing of the hawk and his friend in the water and mist. When the unicorn had nearly given up all hope, he noticed a rainbow appear in the water as it splashed off the rocks in the strange sunlight of Thunderlandia. For all unicorns, the sight of a rainbow in times of distress is a sign of hope. Silverthorne remembered Paddy's shamrock and its message of faith, hope, love and luck. Just before Paddy Cornelius O'Shaughnessey fell onto the rocks, the strong beak of the once Evil Hawk snatched the little gnome from behind, reversed course and flew Paddy up and away to safety on the river bank far above the waterfall. Just as he had promised, the hawk repaid Paddy in his greatest time of need.

Although shaking from the scare of his life and the soaking of a lifetime, Paddy lay on the mountainside and calmed himself, collected his wits and marveled at his good fortune. Was it the luck of the unicorn? Or did Good King Brendon's words on their parting have new meaning now?

Certainly Paddy's past kindness to both the unicorn and the hawk seemed to be paying off. Now he must depend on the luck of the unicorn for what was in store for them ahead. Once again Paddy found himself bidding farewell to his friend, the once Evil Hawk.

After collecting their belongings and finding dry clothing, Paddy and Silverthorne resumed their journey toward Thunderlandia. As they climbed over a mountainous crag and looked below to the rope bridge, they saw the Wicked Wizard Lizard and the Snafferjabber still hanging on for their miserable lives. The bridge still rocked out of control as they howled hideously at each other. Even at their safe distance, Paddy felt shivers down his spine. It was comforting for the gnome and the unicorn to know that those two would not bother them again. Once again, the two travelers marveled at their good luck in overcoming frightful obstacles. Hot buttered babies, indeed!

Chapter Ten:

Once There Was a Two-Headed Thunder Lizard and Fearless Vampire Bats

P addy and Silverthorne had no map or means to calculate the final leg of their incredible journey. After climbing rocky slopes for hours, they entered a dark thicket of thorns and nettles that seemed endless, skirting a winding bend of jagged rocks on a treacherous path. Then they wandered aimlessly for days in the mist and rain. Each day became more dreary and grim than the one before. When they were exhausted and felt unable to go further, they stepped into a clearing and stood in the shadow of Thunder Mountain. It was an ugly, ominous rock edifice that reached to the sky. Nothing green grew near its base—no trees, no shrubs, and no plants of any sort—only a nondescript mass of rubble, rock and dirt surrounded it.

Legend said that when the dim sunlight of Thunderlandia caught the mountain just right at sunrise or sunset, the empty eyes of a skull glared at visitors who dared approach. It was common knowledge that the mountain was full of tunnels and caverns. Deep inside, at the bleak heart of the mountain, lay the lair of the Heathen Banshee, protected by her loyal subjects.

The Heathen Banshee, whose real name was Snagnasty (known to some as Old Snag), was a mean-spirited, miserable old hag with a black heart and a bad attitude. As Paddy Cornelius O'Shaughnessey stood in the shadow of Thunder Mountain, he began to shudder at his memory of the vile banshee and her skilled army of warriors. The hag and her minions had swept over the land of Good King Brendon's forefathers and ancestors.

Even though the ancient gnome king was able to gather his warriors together and mount a formidable defense, it was nonetheless a bloody and terrible battle. Eventually the Heathen Banshee and her army were defeated. Bloody and broken, most of them scattered in mutiny, but those few who remained loyal to the hag, mostly out of fear, were driven along with Old Snag across the Raging River through the Wild Lands and ultimately to Thunder Mountain. Taking refuge inside the dark corridors of the mountain, the wretch resisted further assaults from the forces of good by posting her pets, the Fearless Vampire Bats, at the entrances to all the tunnels. Paddy worried about those Fearless Vampire Bats now.

Paddy remembered now the tales he had heard of how the Good King Brendon drove Snagnasty across the Raging River through fierce hand-to-hand combat with the banshee. Brendon fought with sword and dagger, while the Heathen Banshee used black magic and treachery. The brave gnome was able to subdue Snagnasty by driving his dagger into her eye, thinking he'd blinded her. Paddy had felt the great power of that dagger when he'd once held it.

Brendon's assault on the Heathen Banshee left her bitter, wicker, and with only one eye. Paddy understood that by staring into a mirror the old crone could conjure black magic. Naturally, he wondered what further evil was in store for him and Silverthorne. Worse yet, since Snagnasty now possessed the Magic Box, darkness had descended on the little gnome's world, adding fear and confusion to his thoughts. Paddy knew he must push aside his fears and begin his climb up Thunder Mountain,. So he touched his breast and felt the shamrock in his pocket. This small gesture comforted him now. Still, Paddy and Silverthorne needed to find a way into the heart of the mountain to reverse the Heathen Banshee's frightening spell over all the land. Reclaiming the Magic Box for the Good King Brendon would ensure that.

With amazing luck and great surprise the two discovered an unguarded entrance to one of the tunnels into the mountain. Luckily, there were no nasty bats anywhere to be seen. They crept into the disgusting hole and commenced the final part of their journey, which they hoped would fulfill their mission.

An eternity seemed to pass as Paddy and Silverthorne blindly burrowed deeper and deeper into the mountain. Fatigued and fearing they were hopelessly lost, the two were about to give up and turn back when they noticed a dim light glowing against the cavern wall. Encouraged, but still wary, they crept quietly onward, watching, as the light grew more brilliant. Could they be on the right track after all? They pushed forward.

Soon they heard a faint rumbling sound. Not long after, the tunnel led them to the source of the light and strange sound. Moving quickly along the rocky way, Paddy

and Silverthorne soon stumbled into a giant cavern lit by scores of large candles, the whole room flanked by a roaring fire in a huge hearth. The room was very warm. What amazed them most was the brilliance caused by the light from the fire and candles reflecting off the enormous piles of gold coins and jewels that filled the cavern. The shining gold and sparkling gems created the light that guided them through the dark tunnels of the mountain. The sight astonished the weary travelers, and they turned to stare at one another, then at the piles of riches.

Just behind them they saw the source of the strange rumbling sound that echoed through the tunnel. There in the center of a pile of priceless jewels lay that brutal beast of a dragon, the Two-Headed Thunder Lizard—fast asleep! The strange sound broadcast through the tunnel was the dragon's snoring.

And what a stench! With every breath the Thunder Lizard took, he spewed a foul odor—rancid as death itself. Staring at the two maws of the beast, Paddy noticed hundreds of sharp, twisted teeth exposed from his slack jaws. Even in the warm room, Paddy shivered, for between the two heads of this slumbering beast, amid swirling tendrils of putrid mist from its two mouths...lay the Magic Box.

Even after traveling many miles and surviving trials and near destruction by their wits and luck, Paddy had never actually formulated a plan to retrieve the box, once they'd found it. Now he and the unicorn stood but a few feet from their goal and had no idea how to lay their hands upon it. Paddy decided they must steal the box then and there! There was no point plotting or planning now. They had to take advantage of this

situation. The Thunder Lizard was asleep, there were no bats in sight, and perhaps the banshee didn't even know of their presence. Yet Paddy was sure that they would soon be discovered.

Until now, Paddy and Silverthorne had been lucky to penetrate the depths of Thunder Mountain without being detected. They knew that the Heathen Banshee's Fearless Vampire Bats guarded the mountain to ensure that no one entered, and if they did, that they would not leave. The gnome was sure that they would appear, even if all went well. Yes, it was best to act now, and quickly.

The two began scrambling up the mound of gold and gems, careful not to rouse the dragon. Nonetheless, the four eyes of the two heads snapped open! One of the heads reared up ferociously, while the other appeared groggy and confused. Paddy had heard stories of how one of the heads of the beast was intelligent, cunning and pure evil while the other was stupid, dull and easily duped. Scholarly and learned gnomes who dabbled in science and wizardry referred to the creature as schizoid, for although it had but one body, it was two very different beings. Paddy now realized what that meant. The shrewd head moved menacingly, like a snake ready to strike, glaring with cruel and hideous eyes. The dumb head blinked incoherently and seemed to wonder where it was.

Paddy, a true Irish gnome, tried to sweet-talk the two heads to offer diversion, while Silverthorne grabbed the Magic Box and escaped to the tunnel they had just entered. The evil head began to blow smoke, and flames flared from its nostrils, as it tried to fry Paddy and Silverthorne into crispy critters then and there—instant dinner. Nevertheless, Paddy kept talking nonsense, for gnomes do that best during a crisis. Perhaps the cheap talk could buy them time. The schmoozing was working on the dumb head, but the shrewd head, which was as loathsome as a dragon could be, wanted to fry and eat. Talk was cheap and pointless. After all, dragons don't chit-chat with their next meal.

Grasping wildly at straws, Paddy recalled the words of his sage king and pulled out his glistening harp. For a moment the evil head stopped its menacing movements and stared at the shiny object. Paddy began to pluck and strum. Picking up on this, the unicorn chimed in with his sweet voice. To their complete surprise, the friends discovered they could mesmerize the deadly beast. As Paddy played his magnificent instrument, Silverthorne sang songs never before heard by the creature. Like the Terrible Orcs before them, the soothing voice of the unicorn soon made the Thunder Lizard's four eyelids heavy, quickly putting it to sleep. Paddy then snatched the Magic Box and bolted for the tunnel with his precious cargo.

The song of the unicorn and the melody of the harp echoed through the tunnels and caverns in Thunder Mountain. This was the domain of the Heathen Banshee, and music was never heard here. Ever suspicious, Snagnasty investigated. The old hag entered the giant cavern just as the gnome and the unicorn ducked into a tunnel on the other side of the room of gold and jewels. The Heathen Banshee gasped as she saw that they had the Magic Box! On seeing her trusted and beloved Thunder Lizard fast

asleep, she exploded with rage. Both its heads had gone out like a light, and the beast snored almost peacefully.

Predictably, Old Snag began yelling and screeching at the top of her leathery lungs: "You fools!"

Her shrill voice snapped both of the dragon's heads awake. The beast's hideous skulls swayed, groggy and out of control, smacking into each other like rocks in a sack, causing further disorientation. Frantic, Snagnasty ran around pulling her hair and shrieking: "You fools, you fools, after them! They have the precious box."

The Thunder Lizard reared up on its four legs, wobbly at first, and charged recklessly for the tunnel the two friends had just darted into. The Heathen Banshee ran after the lizard, still screaming, "Breathe fire, and burn them!" She summoned her Fearless Vampire Bats, screeching, "Come to me at once—where are you? Seek them, savage them, my pets!"

She summoned her
Fearless Vampire
Bats, screeching,
"Seek them, savage
them, my pets!"

Chapter Eleven:

Once There Was a Most Horrible Ruckus
Inside Thunder Mountain

Paddy Cornelius O'Shaughnessey hopped onto Silverthorne's back, and off they disappeared into the darkness of the tunnel, as fast as the tiny unicorn's legs could go. The Two-Headed Thunder Lizard was in hot pursuit, the evil head growling and snorting fire and putrid plumes of smoke, which filled the tunnel with disgusting fumes. The dumb head was wheezing and coughing, trying to be fearsome, but it choked and spewed flames that merely singed the hair of the evil head. This caused aggravation and quarreling between the two lizard heads, a laughable sight under any other circumstance. From a fork in the tunnel the Heathen Banshee appeared with her bats flying behind. Paddy and Silverthorne raced down another tunnel, not knowing for sure if the way they were now heading would lead to safety or a dead end.

The Two-Headed Thunder Lizard spewed a ribbon of fire just as the heroes dodged into the tunnel, and the fire shot straight toward Old Snag, scorching her already ugly face and scraggly hair. Snagnasty howled in misery, and her fury rose. The tunnel shook with her rage. Now more hideous than ever with a charred face and

singed hair, the hag pounded both heads of the Thunder Lizard. She hollered to her precious Fearless Vampire Bats, "Seek them. Savage them!" Her screams echoed through the depths of Thunder Mountain and terrified Paddy and Silverthorne, as they continued galloping in the darkness, trusting blindly that escape was possible.

The Heathen Banshee then climbed onto the back of the Thunder Lizard. Using her snake as a whip, she lashed at the dragon mercilessly. Smarting from the fangs of the angry snake, the lizard fled in reckless pursuit of the two thieves. On command, the Fearless Vampire Bats joined in the chase, flying ahead at breakneck speed. The one-eyed banshee yelled her encouragement, "Get them, my fiends!"

Paddy Cornelius O'Shaughnessey and Silverthorne the Unicorn rounded a corner and nearly crashed headfirst into a stonewall, where their worst fears came true. It was a dead end, and all the forces of evil were at their heels. Panicked, the two friends trembled and awaited their fate. Silverthorne's knees began to knock. The Fearless Vampire Bats were quickly closing in on them; they could hear the wings flapping. That, plus the screams and roars and flames from the Two-Headed Thunder Lizard caused horrendous echoes in the darkness. Paddy gasped on seeing the bats' tiny red eyes closing in on the two of them.

A strange heat filled the small cavern from the flames of the Two-Headed Thunder Lizard's four nostrils, and the stench from the beast was overwhelming. Each time the giant Two-Headed Thunder Lizard took a step, the ground beneath them all shook, and rocks, dirt and rubble fell from above. The banshee screamed furiously above the din, which alternated with the wails from the dragon when the fangs of the snake bit into its rump. Paddy and Silverthorne then saw Snagnasty's hideous face, blackened by soot, and her crazy eye, glazed with purest malice. Once again she shrieked, "Destroy them, you fiends!"

The Fearless Vampire Bats were now upon them. What was to become of Paddy and Silverthorne? Were they doomed? Paddy wracked his brain for an idea, any idea. There was something he was forgetting. But what was it?

Paddy and Silverthorne then saw Snagnasty's hideous face, blackened by soot, and her crazy eye, glazed with purest malice...

Chapter Twelve:

Once There Was the Power of the Shamrock

The two friends feared a bleak end was near, when suddenly Paddy remembered the shamrock! In the final frantic moments before the bats came close enough to attack, Paddy focused his gaze sharply in the darkness. The glowing eyes of the Fearless Vampire Bats were close enough now that Paddy could see their sharp fangs and smell their dreadful breath. It was the same scent of evil he smelled on the banshee. Paddy pulled the shamrock from his vest pocket and thrust it high into the air. The shamrock glowed as he pointed it toward the winged creatures. To Paddy's surprise, they stopped in mid-flight, crashing into one another as they avoided the glorious power of the tiny leaves. For once, the Heathen Banshee's fearless pets felt fear—a strange sensation for them—and they flew into one another in desperate retreat. Meanwhile, the Two-Headed Thunder Lizard came full force toward Paddy, its bulk causing the tunnel walls to shudder as each foot slammed to the ground.

The Heathen Banshee was still astride the Thunder Lizard, her snake coiled around her arm, its fangs biting the dragon's rump to increase its speed. Just in the nick of time both heads of the Thunder Lizard ducked to avoid the retreating bats, which smacked into Old Snag headfirst at full speed. Wailing in surprise and pain, Snagnasty and her pet snake fell off the back of the Thunder Lizard. Both serpent and old Snag crashed to the ground of the tunnel, where she cracked the back of her ugly skull.

Suddenly, everything grew calm. The bats were gone, the Heathen Banshee lay on her back with an aching head, and the dragon stumbled about, as the dust settled around them all. Paddy stared at the shamrock in awe. He admired its beauty and brilliance and marveled at its ability to turn back fierce beasts. Silverthorne worried that Paddy was slipping into a trance, and he worried about how soon the Heathen Banshee would wake from her stupor. So the little unicorn frantically searched for an escape route. He used the same lucky brilliance that Paddy used to turn away evil, and soon enough, he discovered a small hole in the stone wall. He was certain that it led to the outside. The unicorn woke Paddy from his reverie. Together they could see that the opening might be large enough to squeeze through.

All too soon, the Heathen Banshee pulled herself off the cavern floor. Still groggy, her head aching miserably, she realized the thieves were escaping with the Magic Box. She screamed at the Thunder Lizard to chase down the intruders. The Fearless Vampire Bats were still confused, flying about in opposite directions. The brilliance of the shamrock still lit a part of the cavern, revealing an escape route. The Two-Headed Thunder Lizard arrived just in time to see the tail end of the unicorn squeeze through the opening toward daylight. The two heads dove for the unicorn at the same time,

and the evil head grabbed Silverthorne. The unicorn began to kick and landed a lucky blow to the dragon's snout. Smarting from the blow, The Two-Headed Thunder Lizard jerked its evil head up and banged itself on the rocks above, then slammed into the dumb head, knocking them both silly. By now Silverthorne was free, and he and Paddy pushed through the tiny hole into a narrow tunnel that led outside.

Still terrified from the whole ordeal inside Thunder Mountain, Paddy and Silverthorne wasted no time scampering through the small space toward the dim light ahead. In their haste they stumbled on the loose rocks and tree roots. They fell and tumbled head over wooden clogs and tiny hooves out into the dull gray sunlight of Thunderlandia. Although definitely not the sunny blue sky of his beloved ancient forest back home, Paddy welcomed the pewter sky, and tears of happiness welled up in his green eyes.

In the commotion of their escape, Paddy had dropped the Magic Box, and it lay nearby, its lid slightly open. The little gnome noticed a strange mist coming from the box. Paddy Cornelius O'Shaughnessey remembered the stern but kindly warning of the Good King Brendon: "Never open or look inside the Magic Box." Slowly, Paddy felt the power of the box as if it beckoned him to peer inside it. The temptation was great, overwhelming him, and his resistance weakened.

Paddy Cornelius O'Shaughnessey crawled slowly on his knees to the Magic Box. He gently cradled it in his arms. The mist from the box encircled his head, filling his senses. Paddy closed his eyes and instantly felt a wish for power, wealth and fame. He

opened his eyes and firmly but quietly snapped the lid shut. The Magic Box was secure at last, its awesome mysteries safely locked inside. Paddy Cornelius O'Shaughnessey remained the loyal, faithful and obedient servant his king knew he would be. And it was confirmed in the wink of an eye.

Meanwhile, the dumb head of the Two-Headed Thunder Lizard popped through the opening of the tunnel, its jaws snapping viciously at Paddy and Silverthorne, but the beast became stuck! It couldn't come closer, nor could it pull its head back back through the opening and into the tunnel. To assure their safety, the two heroes resorted to an old trick. Silverthorne broke into song and, after securing the Magic Box, Paddy strummed his harp. The music lulled the dragon into a deep sleep.

Inside the cavern the Heathen Banshee discovered that the two thieves had escaped from Thunder Mountain with the Magic Box. She began beating the giant beast with her fists to wake the Thunder Lizard from its slumber and make chase. Yet the dragon remained fast asleep, snoring hoarsely. The opening was fully blocked. Frustrated, Old Snag began pulling her frazzled hair and pounding the stone walls of Thunder Mountain, cursing her fate. She had once again lost the Magic Box.

Wasting no time, Paddy and Silverthorne collected themselves and dashed down the side of Thunder Mountain. Behind them they could hear the hag screaming in her mountain lair. Snagnasty's minions had failed her in her time of need, had failed to fry the intruders, and the Magic Box was no more in Thunder Mountain.

Chapter (Lucky) Thirteen

Once There Was a Time When They All
Lived Happily Ever After

Even though Paddy and Silverthorne still had to travel the long and dangerous road back through Thunderlandia and the Wild Lands before reaching home, the worst was over at last. They had the Magic Box, and that would keep danger at bay. Old Snag and her terrible powers were strong for sure, but they were less powerful outside Thunder Mountain. Even more comforting was the fact that Snagnasty no longer had the Magic Box. The friends knew that it would take a long time to rouse the slumbering Thunder Lizard, whose head plugged the hole in the mountain. Furthermore, her Fearless Vampire Bats had all scattered every which way. Such circumstances offered them a healthy head start toward home.

To be sure, the two heroes encountered other adventures. One involved a damsel in distress, the beautiful Phoebe Fiona. While saving her from dire peril, Paddy discovered that she filled his heart, his very being, with her love, a love he had never before experienced, and it brought him incredible peace. Paddy felt his love for Phoebe Fiona inside him like a fire that would never cease to burn. The beautiful

Phoebe Fiona consumed Paddy's thoughts and inspired in him new hopes and dreams. Because of her, the little gnome never expected to feel loneliness or melancholy again.

At the end of his journey, when Paddy Cornelius O'Shaughnessey arrived at his humble home in the ancient forest, life was once again as it should be. Peace and prosperity had been restored to that faraway land of long ago. On his very first day home, Paddy visited his special perch on the cliffs overlooking the majestic sea. He sat quietly and reflected with joy and gratitude on how wonderful his life had become. Indeed, on that same day he shared the wonder of his rose garden and the special rose named Love's Promise with his beautiful Phoebe Fiona. She watched Paddy clip and tend his flowers, and both Phoebe and Paddy knew in their hearts that they would live happily ever after.

As for Silverthorne the Unicorn, his friendship with Paddy Cornelius O'Shaughnessey grew and prospered, and it was treasured always and forever by the both of them. For somewhere along the long and winding road back from Thunderlandia, the two heroes realized the depth of their friendship, perhaps because they had time to reflect on how they had vanquished great danger by using the combined power of their wits, their hearts, and a little luck. The reluctant little gnome and the shy silly unicorn had at last achieved success on their noble mission. As the Good King Brendon had known and said to Paddy: in the good, kind and honest heart dwells an uncommon courage. And to be sure, the best weapons against all that is fearsome in

this sometimes scary world are always faith, hope, love—and a little luck. Small surprise, then, that Paddy Cornelius O'Shaughnessey and Silverthorne the Unicorn had returned safe and sound from their quest with that most precious treasure, the Good King Brendon's Magic Box.

The End